CW00521018

BEDSIDE
Kama Sutra

BEDSIDE

Kama Sutra

Linda Sonntag

hamlyn

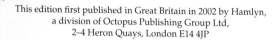

This edition first published in Great Britain in 2002 by Hamlyn,
a division of Octopus Publishing Group Ltd,
2–4 Heron Quays, London E14 4JP

ISBN-13: 978-0-600-60598-0
ISBN-10: 0-600-60598-1

A CIP catalogue record for this book is available at the
British Library

The material in this book has been adapted from
The Photographic Kama Sutra previously published by Hamlyn

Warning
With the prevalence of AIDS and other sexually transmitted diseases,
if you do not practise safe sex you are risking both your health
and that of your partner.

CONTENTS

Introduction

In ancient India, as in many other places in the ancient world, sex was celebrated and explored without shame.

Sometime between the first and fourth centuries AD in Benares, a holy sage called Vatsyayana, about whom little else is known, wrote down everything he could discover about the sexual practices of his countryfolk in a meticulous guide to sexual etiquette called the *Kama Sutra*. His work is more a treatise than a pillow book – its title translates as 'the science of pleasure'. The sage dedicated his researches to the goddess from whom all ecstasy flows. The *Kama Sutra* mirrors the privileged world that Vatsyayana lived in, a world saturated with indolence, luxury and intrigue. The main objective of upper class Indian society was the pursuit of pleasure, and its obsessions were seduction and sex. Amoral and materialistic as this world may have been, it also reached a spiritual dimension, and sex was the gateway to achieving it.

Experiences that transcend time and place bring a deep happiness and fulfilment that put everyday problems into perspective. They enable us to tap into a well of generosity and deal lightly and kindly with the world. Emotionally committed sex provides one way of experiencing the transcendent. The ancient Indian sages found that yoga provides another. Yoga

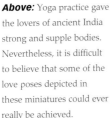

Above: Yoga practice gave the lovers of ancient India strong and supple bodies. Nevertheless, it is difficult to believe that some of the love poses depicted in these miniatures could ever really be achieved.

and sex together form the basis of Tantrism, or spiritual sex. Yoga means literally 'yoke' – it is said to have been invented by the god Shiva, Lord of the Dance, to join himself in sex to the fundamental creative power of the ultimate goddess, Kali. The Tantrists believed that women possess more spiritual energy than men, and that men could join themselves to the divinity only through sacred, highly charged emotional sex with a woman.

The love positions presented in original photographic sequences in the *Bedside Kama Sutra* and depicted in the exquisite Indian miniatures featured in the book have all been inspired by yoga. For some of the sequences in this book, the lovers need to be strong, graceful and supple. Practice in yoga will benefit all the poses, as well as enhancing self-awareness, increasing vitality and improving your ability to relax. Introduce yourselves gradually to the poses, use them as inspiration for your own sexual journey and avoid forcing anything that does not come naturally. May the goddess be with you!

Centre
Yourself

YOGA PRACTICE

Yoga is the world's most ancient system of personal development. It means the joining of the body and the consciousness to an unchanging reality that lies beyond. Yoga allows you to float free of personal worries and leave the clutter of everyday life behind. It strengthens and tones the body, improving the functioning of muscles and joints. The spine grows more flexible and the exercises also work on the internal organs, the glands and the nerves. The physical and emotional effects of yoga open your mind and body to deeper sexual feelings.

YOGA AND SEX

Yoga can help with sex because it is difficult to get in tune with your partner if one of you is distracted or tense. You both need to be centred – in touch with yourselves – before you can connect with each other. Yoga can help you relax. It is possible to be tense all the time without realizing it, even to lie rigidly in bed, grimly awaiting sleep with your mind and body galvanized for the sound of the alarm clock and the next headlong dash into action. Try tensing and relaxing your muscles to see just how keyed up you are.

Physical relaxation brings a feeling of wellbeing, as well as freedom from aches and pains, but yoga gives more than this. As you continue to practise it, yoga brings a sense of the harmony and peace of mind that are the foundations of true self-knowledge. It provides a touchstone of relaxation and stillness that will always enable you to get your bearings in the confusion of everyday life.

YOGA POSTURES

The exercise of yoga consists of getting into and out of a series of postures, or *asanas*. The movements are slow and graceful, never jerky. They extend your reach gradually and should not be forced. After a yoga session, you should feel relaxed and full of energy, not exhausted or strained. Deep, measured breathing is important to help you move correctly.

When you start following the sequences in this book, you may find some of the positions difficult to get into, unless you are already practising yoga. Don't push yourselves to do anything that is uncomfortable, or hurts. Just imagine forming the shapes in the photographs

even if you can't achieve them. With practice, you will become more supple. Alternatively, use the positions shown here as an inspiration for your own individual sequence of movements.

THE BREASTS

The breast is the source of the baby's first nourishment, the milk of human kindness. Breasts stand for comfort, compassion, security and plenty, intimacy and protection. They are also powerful sexual symbols. 'In our maturer years,' wrote Darwin, 'when an object of vision is presented to us which bears any similitude to the form of the female bosom … we feel a general glow of delight which seems to influence all our senses, and if the object be not too large we experience an attraction to embrace it with our lips as we did in early infancy the bosom of our mothers.'

Only one-third of the breast tissue is concerned with milk production. The firm rounded shape has everything to do with sexual signalling. Yet the two functions, to attract and to feed, are inextricably meshed in the mind. A fascinating piece of research into the behaviour of American soldiers in the Vietnam War showed that the closer they were to the battle zone, the more bare-breasted pin-ups they displayed – and the more milk they drank. In a life-threatening situation, the GIs craved a return through sex to the safety of their mother's breast.

COMFORT AND LOVE

Bosom friends, the bosom of the family, returning to the bosom of the earth, all these phrases show the strong connection between the chest, which houses the heart, and a feeling of origin and end, home and belonging. To cuddle close and lay

12

Above. Shiva dreamily contem
plates his consort's beauty while
caressing her breasts. They seem
to arouse in him a special degree
of tenderness.

your head on your partner's chest in a secure embrace is a
potent antidote to worry and stress. It is a taste and a memory
of the unconditional love in which we imagine we basked as
babies. In holding and being held and loved, we relax and
revive into a stronger sense of self.

LOOKING AFTER YOUR BREASTS

The breasts extend from the second to the sixth rib and are
composed of milk glands encased in fatty tissue. They are
supported by suspensory ligaments called the ligaments of
Ashley Cooper, which give them their line and lift. Breasts are at
their fullest and perkiest at around age 22, the optimum age for

reproduction in a woman's life when she is most likely to bring a foetus to full term. Gravity, lack of support and ageing are the biggest enemy of firm breasts. Because they have no muscles, exercise does little to preserve shape and tone. Nevertheless, activities such as swimming and dancing strengthen the underlying pectoral muscles and give good posture and a sense of wellbeing. A massage from your lover using warm oil and gentle caressing strokes is both relaxing and stimulating. It can be a prelude to making love, or drifting off to sleep – or both!

A NOTE ON SIZE

As with other sexual organs, the size of the breasts doesn't matter. Big or small they function equally well as milk providers. But to a baby suckling at its mother's breast, the breast is enormous, physically and in terms of its importance. This helps to explain the visual appeal to some men of breasts that have been enlarged by plastic surgery to unnatural sizes. They may be pumped full of silicone and hard to the touch, but their sheer size triggers fantasies of comfort and bliss.

BREAST EXERCISE

Here is an exercise for the chest for warmth, generosity and openness. Position yourself with your arms at your sides, then clasp your hands in front of you with arms relaxed. Slowly raise your clasped hands up and lift them high over your head, then let them drop behind it down to the base of your neck. Press your hands together against your back. Bring them slowly back up and over to where you began. Repeat the exercise three times when you get up in the morning.

THE GENITALS

The Tantric sages of ancient India worshipped the goddess Kali, because to them she symbolized the female sex organs, the fount of all life and the most sacred pleasure of living. Kali was also called Cunti and her sign was the yoni or vagina, which was represented by a mouth shape, such as a fish or a double-pointed oval, or by a simple triangle. The triangle was as important to the Tantrists as the cross is to Christians, only of course the triangle symbolizes life and sex, whereas the Christian cross symbolizes death.

THE YONI

The yoni is the symbol of a gateway to secret knowledge and the buried treasure of ecstasy. It is both mouth and well, taking and giving. The yoni swallows the lingam and brings forth life. Swallowing the lingam has its terrifying aspect, just as Kali is also a force of darkness and destruction. According to a Muslim proverb, three things on this Earth are insatiable: the desert, the grave and a woman's yoni. The idea of the castrating and all-devouring toothed vagina is present in all mythologies and reveals the deep male fear of losing himself in an ocean of love and desire, the birth trauma the wrong way round.

The mouth and vagina have many connections. The word mouth comes from the same root as mother. Yawn comes from yoni. The yoni has labiae – lips – and men have feared that, when bared, these lips might reveal teeth. Until recently the male fear of castration led to the belief in many parts of the

THE PELVIC TILT

The pelvic tilt is a primitive dance step much used in belly dancing. Its message is explicit. Stand with knees flexed, feet comfortably close together, arms held out to the sides with palms upwards. Tighten the buttocks, thrust the pelvis forwards and tilt upwards. Then relax the buttocks and push back. Practise until you can tilt your pelvis forwards and backwards smoothly and effortlessly.

world that a male snake fertilizes the female by putting his head in her mouth and being swallowed alive. The ancients described sexual intercourse in similar terms. To them, the man did not take the woman, but was taken by her. When he ejaculated, the woman consumed his vital fluid. Semen means both seed and food, and consummating a sexual union was tantamount to eating the man. When the woman ate the food of the man, her stomach was seen to swell with pregnancy. For men, every orgasm is a little death, the death – albeit temporary – of the phallus which shrivels after sex.

THE LINGAM

Where goddess-worshippers adore the yoni, god-dominated religions worship the phallus. The Jews of the Old Testament worshipped their own genitals and swore oaths by laying a hand on each other's private parts. Words like 'testimony' and 'testament' derive from the word 'testicles', whose original meaning was witnesses. Phallic symbols are the marks of god-dominated religion. They can be seen in standing stones, columns and towers, and also in guns, missiles and other weapons. Terms like 'big shot', 'hit' and 'score' show how phallus worship can confuse sex and aggression.

Those who worship the yoni like it to be strong and muscular so that it can hug the lingam tightly,

18

pulsating and squeezing it to build up a rhythm without moving any other parts of the body. Or the yoni can remain still while the lingam pulsates. Thus the couple can have exciting Tantric sex while remaining outwardly motionless.

For this kind of sex you need strong pelvic floor muscles. To strengthen them, practise regulating the flow of urine vigorously all the time, slowing it, then forcing it to flow more powerfully. Contract the pelvic floor muscles at least 70 times a day to make them really strong. You can do it at any time, as no one will know. Strengthening the perineum is important after childbirth when these muscles have been severely strained. These exercises will also guard against incontinence in old age. As you contract your muscles, tune in to how much is contracting and where the muscles reach to. Do the exercise in bed with your partner and feel the contractions of each other's perineum with your fingers.

Left: In an unusually graphic depiction of oral sex, the woman is shown sucking her partner's lingam. This practice was not always approved of in ancient India, except when it was performed on men by male masseurs (see page 121).

19

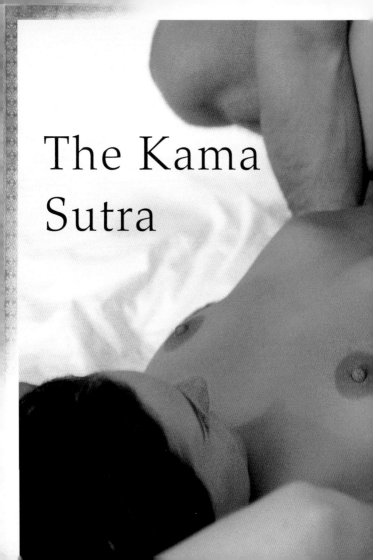

The Kama
Sutra

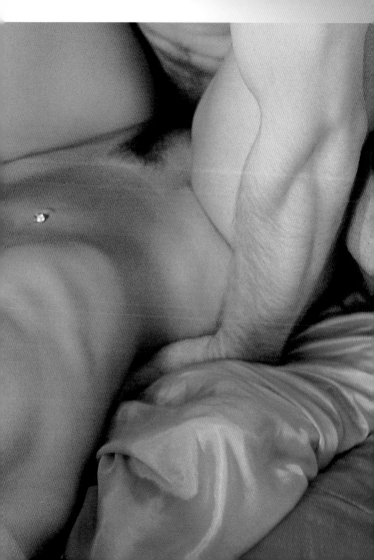

THE FROG

The pleasure here lies in the man keeping up a gentle
rocking motion while the woman stays perfectly still,
moving only the muscles of her yoni to let her partner in
gradually. After a tantalizingly slow build-up, he can
pump vigorously to a climax. The man needs to develop
strong thigh muscles to maintain this position of deep
penetration without tiring. Comfort is important, so if the
strain tells, the man can roll backwards into the sitting
position and let the woman bounce in his lap.

1 First arrange your
cushions. When the
woman lies back, her body
will need to be slightly raised
and a pillow under her
buttocks will allow her
partner deeper entry. The
man squats with legs apart.
The woman sits on his lap,
with her legs over his. In this
position the lovers can kiss
and stimulate each other's
genitals with their hands,
using a massage oil to
enhance the sensation. In this
way, the man can bring his
partner to orgasm.

2 When the time is right, the woman slides her partner's lingam inside her yoni. She will be extra sensitive to the delicious sensation. Clenching and releasing the muscles of her yoni, she begins to rock gently, supporting herself with her arms around her lover's shoulders.

3 The man lowers his partner on to the pillows, sliding his hands down to support the small of her back. In this position he can raise her pelvis towards him and thrust gently, bouncing on his haunches.

Below: Though the man is on top, the woman can still change the mood and the tone of the experience by opening her yoni wider or tilting herself towards or away from him.

COURTESANS

The world's first prostitutes were priestesses who performed sacred sexual rites in the temples. By the time of Vatsyayana, prostitution had moved from the temple to the boudoir, but the Tantric sages still saw sex as a mystic and healing experience and courtesans were held in the highest regard.

The life of a courtesan was in many ways preferable to the life of a wife. Courtesans were usually well-educated women. Witty, amusing, talented and amorous, they were the equals of the interesting and powerful men they attracted and were the only women to enjoy financial and social independence. A clever courtesan would seek out a rich and influential man and set about seducing him. Once the man was snared, she kept his interest by treating him like a god and making herself indispensable while remaining aloof from him in her heart.

CANOPY OF STARS

On a hot summer night, experience the cosmic bliss of
Tantra under the stars. Walk out with your lover to a
secret moonlit place. Spread a thick rug on the ground and
lay a pillow at either end. Feel the earth move with you as
comets explode, trailing fiery showers above.

1 The man sits down on the
rug, stretching his legs out
in front of him and keeping
his back firm and straight.
The woman sits sideways
between his legs with her legs
and feet together along his
left hip. They embrace, she
around his shoulders and he
around her hips.

2 Leaning back, the
woman supports herself
with her right hand on the
rug. She curls her right leg
tightly round her lover's
waist. Then, slowly, she lifts
her left foot in her left hand
like a dancer, straightening

her leg and pointing her foot
over his right shoulder. He
leans back to allow her leg to
pass in front of his face, then
supports her body under the
small of her back. The pose is
open and provocative, the
moment is mystical.

3 When the moment is right, coitus can begin. The woman lets go of her foot, signalling her readiness, so her left leg lies hard against his shoulder. Her hands are on the ground behind her to support her weight. He clasps her back and draws her on to him. United, the lovers maintain this deeply penetrative pose with little movement until they feel full of each other's presence.

4 Then the man clasps her wrists, she clasps his, and they both lower themselves gently down into the pillows. Her legs slide along his sides, mirroring the pose of his legs. They each raise one arm above their heads in a gesture of openness to the heavens, still clasping each other with the other hand.

Right: In this love pose, gazing into each other's eyes is followed by gazing into heaven to discover the direct experience of ever-lasting power and transcendence. The stars are symbols of the spirit, guiding lights shining in the darkness.

THE COW

This sequence offers an exciting way into a simple
position. The man can thrust vigorously and the woman
can respond by slamming her buttocks into him. Or she
can begin to subside on to a cushion, leading him into a
more gentle lying down position, often referred to in the
West as 'spoons'.

1 The man kneels on the
floor with his knees close
together and his buttocks on
his heels, his feet flat down
behind him. The woman half
kneels down close to him on
his left side. Their bodies are
touching and their arms
caressing one another. She
has her right arm round his
right shoulder and her left
hand on his right forearm.
He has his left arm around
her back and his right hand
on her waist.

2 She lunges her right leg over his thighs, creating a right angle to the floor, making sure that her lunge is deep enough so that her knee does not extend over her foot. She balances on her left knee and her left hand moves to his leg. He supports her right thigh with his right hand.

3 From this position she slides her right leg in a perfectly straight line and extends her left leg behind her until her weight is fully on his body. She points both her feet and balances between her right heel and her left knee. She gently lifts her spine up towards her partner so her back is leaning on his chest and she can twist towards him to gaze lovingly into his eyes.

4 As he enters her, she turns her back to him and bending forwards, rests both hands on the ground. She swings both of her legs back next to his.

5 He clasps her around the waist with both hands, and rising on to his knees, lifts her up and forward until her feet come together in front of his knees. Resting her head on a cushion, she clasps her hands as if in prayer under her cheek.

SHOAL OF FISH

This position is so-named because the woman looks as though she is swimming. She supports her torso on a convenient piece of furniture, such as the back of a couch, and the man moves, first gently and then more vigorously, between her legs.

1 The man puts his left knee on the floor and his right foot on the floor with his right knee at a right angle. The woman sits on his lap facing away from him with her right knee forward and her left knee pointing down to the ground. The man supports her round the waist and she rests her hands on his. In this position he can kiss the nape of her neck and caress her breasts.

2 He holds her by the waist
and she drops her torso
gracefully forwards,
supporting her weight on her
arms on a piece of furniture.

37

3 The man stands up, sliding his hands along his partner's sides to grip her by the thighs and lift her on to his erect lingam. She keeps her legs straight behind her to allow him freedom of movement. The man controls the pace, thrusting first gently and then passionately as both lovers thrill to the depth of penetration this position affords them.

Above: The lovers choose the terrace of a roof garden in the palace for this pose. There is a special freedom in making love outside.

THE NAILS

The *Kama Sutra* instructs lovers on how to 'press with the nails'. Vatsyayana constructed an elaborate language of erotic scratching, which left marks that could be flaunted as sexual trophies alongside love bites. For this purpose, lovers were advised to keep their nails clean and glossy and to stain them tawny with henna. Appropriate times to mark a lover included during leave-taking before a journey, after returning home, on becoming reconciled after a quarrel, and whenever a woman became intoxicated. Nails could be pressed into the lover's armpits, throat, breasts, lips, midriff, buttocks and thighs and the marks left behind were worn with pride by young women. Men were warned, however, not to mark married women in this way. Married women could bear secret marks only on their private parts, which they could contemplate while sighing with longing for the absent lover.

CHARIOT

For this highly erotic pose, make sure the woman sits on a
cushion to bring her up to a comfortable height, and that
she also has plenty of soft pillows to lean on. Chariot is a
delicate balancing act that needs strong leg muscles to
prevent the couple tiring and a sense of strain taking over
from the ecstasy of contact through just the hands and
genitals. The lovers gaze into each other's eyes to deepen
the sensation of blissful intimacy.

1 The man squats with his
knees turned outwards.
His back is straight. His
partner sits on a cushion in
between his legs, with her legs
over his and her knees
clasping his waist. Her feet
are soles-together behind his
back. She puts her arms
round his back and he holds
her tenderly by the waist.

2 Now the woman leans
back, supporting her
weight by gripping his arms.
She slides her hands down his
arms, then rests her palms on
the ground behind her.

41

3 The woman lifts first her
right leg, then her left,
over her partner's shoulders.
The man stretches his arms
out behind him with palms
flat on the floor and mirrors
the woman's movement,
putting his feet on her
shoulders. This is the
moment of entry.

4 The couple now clasp
forearms under the man's
knees, as he lowers his feet
to the floor.

5 The woman leans back and lowers her feet to the floor over the man's hips and under his arms. They rock gently in a see-saw motion.

Below: The endless variety and richness of repeat patterns on fabrics, wall hangings and carpets says much about the Eastern way of life. The seamlessness of Indian art and music is found again in India's attitude to love: the emphasis is on the continuum, not on beginnings and endings.

SEX AIDS

Dildoes were common sex aids in ancient India. They were often fashioned in the form of a sheath to be worn over the lingam and increase its size. They were made of precious materials, such as gold, silver and ivory, and sometimes of wood, tin or lead. The consequences of rubbing the delicate mucous membranes of the vagina with poisonous lead do not bear thinking about. For solitary pleasure or mutual use in the harem, women used bulbous gourds or roots, well oiled, or bundles of reeds tied together and softened with the extracts of certain plants.

In southern India there was a strong fashion for piercing. In fact it was believed that women could not get true sexual pleasure unless their partner had a ring or a heron bone attached to his lingam.

FEEDING THE PEACOCK

The title of this love pose comes from the Indian miniature shown on page 49, in which the woman holds out a golden cup for the male peacock to peck out of, while her lover's lingam is inside her. The peacock's beak is a metaphor for the lingam, and the gold cup stands for the yoni. Lovers have to be the right height to achieve the pose illustrated in the miniature, but if they are not, the woman can stand on a bench or on the bottom step of a flight of stairs. This pose is one that can be adopted in a hurry, for example while out for a country walk, in which case a tree would provide useful support.

1 A good way to get into the simple standing pose is for the woman to sit with her legs apart on a piece of furniture, such as the back of a sofa, so that she is slightly higher than her partner's genitals. The man squats on his haunches between his partner's legs, from where he can kiss her breasts. She can bend to kiss his mouth.

2 When the time is right, the man stands and lifts his partner on to his lingam. She holds on firmly with her hands around his neck and shoulder and grasps his waist with her thighs. In this position the couple can have vigorous intercourse. The woman moves strongly against her partner, while he supports her bottom with his arms, helping to thrust her against him.

47

3 In this position it is easy to tire. The man can lower his partner gently to the ground, or to a stool or cushion of the right height, so they can stand, still united, 'feeding the peacock'. Stillness is an important part of Tantric sex. It allows exquisite sensations to build up in all the sexual nerve endings, until some kind of movement is urgently required. Now the couple can move very gently, tuning completely into the feelings in their genitals. Finally, when they can stand it no more, the man picks up his partner again and carries her to the couch, where vigorous thrusting is resumed.

Above: Here it is the woman who engages in a diversionary tactic to take her partner's mind off the urgency of sex and make him last longer. If you don't have a peacock to hand, feed your lover grapes. Peel them first of course.

THE PLOUGH

If you are going to try this position on the bed, make sure that it is firm – a soft surface might wobble and upset the lovers' balance. A thick duvet is more comfortable for the man's knees than a bristly carpet. Allow plenty of soft cushions for the woman to rest on. This gentle pose can subside into 'spoons', in which the man rolls over to lie behind his partner, so that both are on their sides, with her fitting into his lap. Spoons is a late-night position, a comforting one in which to fall asleep with the promise of continuing lovemaking in the morning.

1 The man kneels down and the woman sits astride his lap, facing away from her lover. He places his arms around her waist. In this position he can caress her breasts.

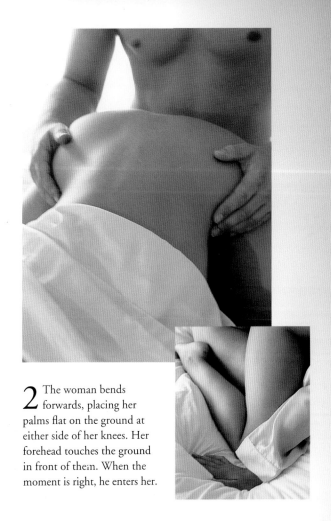

2 The woman bends
  forwards, placing her
palms flat on the ground at
either side of her knees. Her
forehead touches the ground
in front of them. When the
moment is right, he enters her.

3 She stretches her right leg back along the side of his right leg, supporting herself on the ground while keeping her left leg bent. She lowers herself on to the cushions, resting her head on her right arm.

4 Stretching his arms along her back, the man can now rock gently into her. All she has to do is concentrate on the sensations in her yoni, hugging his lingam tightly.

TEMPLE

The Temple is not as difficult as it looks for those with
yoga training who have very supple legs. The final Tantric
pose is outwardly motionless, but the feelings are intense
if the couple have strong pelvic muscle control. Lovers
who are daunted by the exotic leg bends could follow the
instructions as far as Step 2 for a gentle rocking pose that
is easy to achieve.

1 The surface should be
firm – a futon would be
excellent, but most beds are
too soft for this pose, as any
movement would tip the
couple over. The man sits on
the floor with a straight back,
his knees pointing outwards
and the soles of his feet
together. The woman sits
inside his legs, with her legs
round his waist and her soles
together behind him. He
holds her gently round the
waist, while she grips his
back. In this position the
lovers can kiss until they are
well aroused.

2 When the time is right the man lifts his partner up and forwards and penetrates her. She now leans back to support herself with her palms flat on the ground behind her. She lifts her buttocks off the floor and her right leg over his shoulder. She follows with her left leg so that both legs are parallel. The lovers gaze into each other's eyes and the man rocks his partner gently backwards and forwards. Now the man leans back to support his own weight on the floor with palms flat and fingers pointing backwards. He lifts first his right leg and then his left on to her shoulders. In this position the couple can rock gently against one another.

3 The man moves his right leg to the ground and the woman clasps his foot in her right hand. She now drops her left leg to the floor alongside his body. The man holds up his right arm, she raises her left arm and they clasp hands above their heads. If this pose is uncomfortable, the couple can drop both legs to the ground and lean close together to kiss.

IN THE MOOD FOR LOVE

Below: The four-poster bed with its rich canopy and pure white quilt provides the perfect setting for a pose dedicated to the goddess. The Indian lovers surround themselves with a variety of plump cushions for comfort and support.

The student of the *Kama Sutra* receives his beloved in the pleasure room, which is decorated with flowers and heady with perfume, in the company of his friends and servants. The woman enters, freshly bathed and scented, and wearing beautiful robes, jewellery and flowers. She sits at his left hand and he invites her to drink. Touching her hair and the knot of her garment, he embraces her gently while they talk and amuse one another by embarking on subjects not normally discussed in polite society. The assembled company play musical instruments, sing and drink, until the woman is overcome with love and desire. Then at a signal from the citizen, his friends and servants depart, taking with them gifts of flowers, ointments and betel leaves. The two are left alone to celebrate their passion.

THE HUNTER

Hunting was one of the favourite pursuits of upper-class Indians. Some liked to combine it with sex. In this position the Indian prince takes up his rifle to shoot a gazelle (see page 61). Modern-day Western lovers rock gently backwards and forwards. This position is more exciting if all the movement is left to the woman.

1 The lovers stand facing each other. The man drops to his right knee and keeps his left knee up with his foot firmly on the floor at right angles to it. The woman lifts her right leg up and places her right foot delicately on his left hip bone. Her toes point outwards and her heel points to his groin. Her standing leg remains straight.

2 She lowers herself on to his thigh, circling his right shoulder with her left arm. He embraces her, drawing her to him, and they kiss.

59

3 He grips her more tightly around the waist and draws her closely towards him. She puts her right hand on his left knee and her left hand behind his neck to support her balance and pulls herself closer to him. In this position he enters her.

4 She drops down to her left knee and curves her right leg around his waist so their bodies are close, yet balanced away from each other. She points her toes and takes hold of her left foot with her left hand. He draws her body even closer as they gaze directly into each other's eyes.

COURTING

Above: Perhaps the ultimate exercise in warding off premature ejaculation was to transfer the release to a firearm! The modern-day equivalent might be sex while watching football on television.

When a man loves a girl he should sit next to her at parties and gatherings and take every opportunity to touch her. He places his foot on hers and touches each of her toes with his own. If she lets him do this, he takes her foot in his hand and presses her toes with his fingers. If he is a visitor at her house and she is washing his feet, he squeezes one of her fingers between two of his toes, and whenever their eyes meet he looks significantly at her and with longing. As she begins to fall in love with him, he craftily pretends illness and begs her to come to his house. He then persuades her to tend him for three days and three nights, during which time he talks softly to her, letting her into the secrets of his heart.

THE WHEEL

Yoga practice will give the woman the strength, flexibility of spine and stamina she needs for this love pose. The angle of penetration ensures that her G-spot is stimulated, which gives some women heightened pleasure. However practised and supple his partner is, the man should be gentle in this pose, taking care to support the small of her back and avoiding vigorous thrusting. He should also protect his own back by bending at the knees when he lowers her to the ground, and again when he lifts her back up to face him. The couple can continue lovemaking with her arms around his neck.

1 First the woman lies flat on the ground with her feet in line with her hips. She brings her arms up and over her head to place her hands as flat as she can on the floor by her ears. Her fingers should point towards her toes.

2 She inhales and arches her back to lift her hips high off the floor, dropping her head back in line with her arms. This is the Wheel position. The man kneels inside her legs on his left knee. His right foot is flat on the ground and his right knee bent at a right angle.

3 The man holds his partner round the waist to support the small of her back. When she feels comfortable and ready, he lifts her off the ground, bending his knees to protect his own back from the strain of her weight. She wraps her right leg around him, keeping her left foot initially on the ground for support. He can now gently enter her.

4 When the man is standing firmly with straight legs, and can support her weight with his hands under her waist, the woman lifts her left foot off the ground and wraps both her legs round his back. In this highly sensitive position the couple can move very gently against each other.

BUTTERFLY

The potential for movement in the Butterfly position is limited, but this is more than made up for by the intense genital pressure, which makes contractions of the pelvic muscles more strongly felt. The woman leans back to increase the pressure. The man has his right knee raised, which balances her weight and reduces strain on his back. From this position, the couple could move into the Wheel (see page 62).

1 The man kneels on both knees, squatting on his heels with the balls of his feet on the ground. The woman sits astride his lap with her feet on the floor behind him and they kiss and caress.

2 When the moment is right, the man raises his right knee, putting his right foot flat on the floor in front of him. At the same time he lifts his partner with his right arm around her waist and his left hand on her shoulder. She supports her weight on both feet, leaning against his right leg as his lingam enters her yoni.

3 Now she lifts her right leg over his left upper arm and her left leg over his right upper arm. She leans back, clasping her arms round his neck, and he supports her weight against his leg and in his arms. Balance is vital to prevent damage to his back.

Below: A perfect way to enjoy a radiant afternoon. The majestic panorama and gilded weapons tell of wealth and power. They have no need to hide themselves as they own all that they can see.

SEDUCTION

The way to charm a woman, says Vatsyayana, is with romantic conversation. If a man's sweet words fall on deaf ears, he is advised to give the object of his desire some intoxicating substance, carry her off and enjoy her before she has time to come round, then immediately set up the marriage ceremony. Neither should he be afraid of going to even greater lengths. Vatsyayana advises his student to ambush the reluctant woman of his dreams while she is walking in the garden. He should attack and kill her guards, then carry her off and proceed as before. A married woman needs a different approach. Poetic talk of budding leaves will be wasted here. Instead, the citizen should adopt the discreet language of amorous signs: pull on his moustache, make a clicking sound with his fingernails, cause his ornaments to tinkle and bite his lower lip.

SULTAN

In this position the woman is in control – the man is both vulnerable and totally pampered, lying back on cushions with his legs in the air, while she clasps him and bounces gently up and down. Or she can decide to be motionless, gazing into her lover's eyes and using her pelvic floor muscles to alternately grip and release his lingam. Make sure the man's back is comfortable, as the woman is holding on to him to keep her balance, not to support him.

1 The woman sits upright on the bed with her knees pointing outwards and the soles of her feet pointing towards each other in front of her. The man sits inside her legs, with his legs over hers and the soles of his feet together behind her back. He clasps her around the shoulders and she embraces his waist. She puts her feet flat on the bed to support herself. In this position the couple can kiss and arouse each other.

70

2 The man now puts his arms back to lower himself among the cushions, and when he is comfortable, he lifts first his right leg and then his left over his partner's shoulders and rests his ankles on her shoulders at either side of her neck. She clasps her lover to her, with her arms over his uplifted legs and her hands resting on his shins.

3 The woman brings her feet back towards her, and plants them flat on the bed so she is squatting on her haunches. When they are both aroused, she guides his lingam inside her yoni, pressing down on the floor with her feet and lifting her buttocks to receive him.

Below: The sultan lies back, sipping a delicious cordial from a silver goblet, and abandons himself to the attentions of his consort. Note how Indian lovers of both sexes removed all body hair – for hygiene, aesthetics and greater skin-to-skin feel.

VITAL STATISTICS

Vatsyayana classifies lovers according to two systems: genital size and intensity of passion. The male organ, the lingam, he groups into three sizes. Men with small lingams are called hares, those of average size are bulls and the most generously endowed are horses. The corresponding sizes for the female yoni are deer, mare and elephant. The best matches are those between same-sized lingams and yonis. Strength of desire is either small, middling or intense, and again, an equal match is the most favourable.

Vatsyayana says that the first time a man makes love with a woman, he will usually come quickly, then gradually gain more control. But it is the other way round for a woman, who grows more abandoned and orgasmic with time.

73

FRENZY

This position is inspired by Indian paintings that show a physically impossible whirling of lovers' legs in which hips, thighs, calves, ankles and feet go berserk. If you are supple, strong and practised in yoga, try this pose and see where it takes you.

1 The man sits on the ground with his legs straight out in front of him and his back erect. The woman kneels astride his lap, close against him, her knees at his hips and her feet folded under at his knees. She has her hands round his waist; he clasps his behind her back. She rests her forehead lovingly on his brow. When the time is right, he enters her.

2 The man continues to support her waist as the woman leans back to place her palms flat on the ground with her fingers pointing towards her partner. She lifts her left leg gracefully over his right shoulder.

3 Now the man leans back, placing his palms on the ground below his shoulders. He pushes up on his arms to raise his hips and the woman arches her back to lift with him. Her legs open wider, but the right foot remains as a support on the ground.

4 She raises her left leg so
that he can slip his right
leg between her legs, crossing
in front of her and placing his
foot at her right side.

5 The man draws his partner to him. They clasp each other, kissing and rocking in an urgent embrace.

RAJASTHAN

The miniature on page 83 shows two Europeans, a Portuguese naval officer and his lover, practising the Tantric arts in Rajasthan in the latter half of the 17th century. Foreign visitors to India were often enthusiastic exponents of Tantra, though sometimes their clumsy efforts caused amusement among local yogis. The sideways pose shown in the miniature is a comfortable one for beginners, who can achieve it easily from a sitting position. The sequence that follows demonstrates a more advanced version, showing how the pose can be greatly enhanced for lovers experienced in yoga.

1 The man sits on the bed with his back straight and his legs stretched out in front of him. His partner sits sideways on his lap, with her right arm around his shoulder. Her legs are together, with feet pointing behind him. The couple gaze into each other's eyes as he embraces her lovingly.

2 The woman leans back, placing her left hand on his leg to support her weight. She curls her left leg around the man's waist and clasping her right ankle in her right hand, raises her leg gracefully in front of his face, bringing it down to rest on his right shoulder, with toe pointing skywards. The man places his right palm behind him to balance her movement.

82

3 Now the man draws his partner to him with his right arm around her waist and she places her left foot flat on the bed to support herself. This is the moment of entry. The woman puts her right arm around her lover's neck. The couple feel love energy flowing between them.

Above: When in Rajasthan… tourists try love Indian-style, with exotic drinks, weaponry and a view to write home about.

WAYS OF LYING TOGETHER

According to Vatsyayana, couples should lie together according to the fit of their genitals. For the tightest fit to accommodate small genitals on both sides, the woman lies on her back with her buttocks on a pillow. The man should apply oil to her yoni to make entry easy. The next stage for slightly larger genitals is called the yawning position. The woman lies on her back and raises her thighs, bending her legs at the knees. She lowers her knees to the sides. This affords penetration that is both sharp and deep. In the position of the wife of Indra, the largest genitals are accommodated. The woman lies on her back with her buttocks raised, bringing her thighs up to her sides and folding her legs at the knees like a frog.

ANTELOPE

Antelope provides the woman with a gracefully seductive sequence of sliding movements against her partner's body; she will benefit from the strength and suppleness that comes with yoga training. She needs to trust that her partner will support her weight as she lifts off into his arms, and he should protect his back at moments of strain by bending his legs at the knee. This is not the easiest pose, but practice will develop a fluid dance-like style that has its own excitement.

1 The lovers stand facing each other with feet together. The man kneels at his partner's feet with his right knee on the ground and his left knee bent. He clasps her round the waist as she sits on his left thigh and puts her arms round his neck.

2 The man stands slowly, supporting her around the back. She lifts both feet off the ground, clasping her legs firmly behind his back as he stands up.

3 The man now bends forwards to lower his partner in front of him. Clasping her firmly round her back, he lifts her on to his erect lingam, and she pushes against him with her legs to position herself comfortably. In this position both lovers are excited by the limited opportunity for movement.

4 Finally, the man lowers his partner to the ground, and she places her palms on the floor in front of his feet to support herself. In this position, the energy flows between them.

THE HORSE

The woman needs a flexible back to be entirely comfortable with this pose, which demands a certain amount of spine-twisting. The man should take care to be guided in the depth of his thrusting by the receptivity of the woman's yoni – the most comfortable final position for her is with head down resting on her arms and buttocks up, so her back is not hurt when she opens right up to her lover's vigorous enthusiasm.

1 The man kneels on the floor with his legs together, his buttocks on his heels and his toes and the balls of his feet on the floor. His partner kneels at his left, their sides touching, their arms around each other, his round her waist and hers round his head and shoulders.

2 She lunges her left knee over his thighs. He supports her round the waist with his left arm, his right hand encircles her right thigh.

3 In this position the lovers can kiss and the man can caress his partner's genitals.

4 They clasp right hands
and he guides her arm
over her head. She is now
ready to lower herself on to
the pillows.

5 Supporting her hips with both hands, the man now rises up on to his knees, sliding her further forwards into the cushions. In the Horse position, he can thrust more vigorously the more her pelvis is tilted towards him.

Below: This colourful miniature shows the richness and symmetry of the sultan's pleasure garden. Tinkling fountains, shady pavilions and scented bowers were essential props in the art of seduction.

MAGIC POTIONS

The men and women of ancient India had access to a wide variety of potions and charms to help them in their amorous adventures. A man could enlarge his lingam by rubbing it with the bristles of certain insects, then for ten nights rub it with oil, followed by another treatment with the bristly insects. After this, his lingam was so swollen that he had to lie down and let it hang through a hole in the bed, then massage it with cooling ointments. The pain would disappear but the swelling would remain.

A woman could rub ointment into her breasts to make them larger, while a man's sexual vigour could be increased by drinking sugared milk in which he had boiled up a goat's testicle. Other magic recipes guaranteed to bring a woman quickly to orgasm, and to delay ejaculation in a man.

STARFLOWER

The name of this pose comes from the calm elegant shapes the lovers' bodies make as they entwine and subside, like a flower unfolding. Starflower allows the couple to relax after an energetic session of lovemaking. It is a warm and intimate pose that also gives each person the space to remember and savour the sensations they have just shared. In this comforting position it is easy to drift off into a blissful sleep.

1 The man sits on the bed with his back straight and his legs stretched out in front of him. He brings his right knee up and puts his foot flat on the bed, level with his left knee. He leans back and puts his hands behind him to support himself.

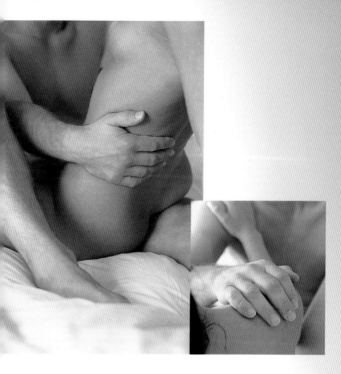

2 The woman sits diagonally on top of her partner with her knees up and her feet flat on the floor. Her left leg is threaded under his right leg. Like him, she leans back with her left arm and supports herself on the floor with her hand. Now he enters her. Their right arms cross, and they put their right hands on each other's right shoulder, gazing calmly into each other's eyes.

4 As their hands part, the man stretches his right leg out to touch the woman's left side. The lovers gently twist their lower bodies towards each other and their upper bodies away, so they are both together and separate, joined, but each looking into his or her own individual world. The woman raises her arms above her head and clasps her hands in a sign of wholeness and satisfaction, while her partner rests his left hand lovingly on her leg.

3 The lovers begin to lower themselves gently on to the bed, letting their hands run down each other's arms as they bend their left elbows and go down on their forearms. The woman slides both her legs out straight either side of her partner.

THE ABDUCTION

The man needs strong leg muscles to carry away his beloved in this dramatic pose, which ends with her nestling among cushions, secure in his arms. If other means failed to win a bride, Vatsyayana recommended abduction. If the girl was a virgin, her lover would be prepared to wait days to gain her confidence before the union was consummated. If the woman was married, on the other hand, her suitor might have to take his life in his hands and murder her husband, before carrying her off into the woods, which is the story told in this sequence.

1 The man stands tall, then lunges into the dramatic Warrior pose, bringing his left leg forward so it is bent at right angles at the knee, and leaving his right leg stretched far behind him. His right foot is at right angles to his body for extra grip and support, while his left foot points forwards. His arms are at his sides. Balance is all important, and this simple move needs plenty of practice if it is to be achieved gracefully.

2 The woman, who has been standing nearby ready to meet her destiny, now places her right foot on his left upper thigh and her left arm around his shoulders in an attitude of sexual acceptance. He gazes into her eyes, placing his left hand under her bended right knee and his right arm around her waist. She puts her arms around him in affirmation.

4 When they are perfectly balanced, she lifts her left leg off the ground and clasps it around his back. She should weigh only lightly on his leg as he maintains this powerful dynamic pose. He can enter her now.

3 Now with his help she swings her body round as though mounting a horse for the getaway. She sits astride his left leg, supporting herself on the ground with her left foot, and embracing her lover in her arms. She curls her right leg around him and he holds her lower back with both his hands.

5 In the final stage of Abduction, the man lowers his lover to the pile of cushions. It is crucial here to avoid back strain, so he should bear her weight on his leg as he lets her down, drawing up his right leg parallel with his left. Gripping her arms in his, he is in a position to rock backwards and forwards into her.

ADULTERY

Above: The prince has his way with the young girl he has brought back to his palace. When their union has been consummated he will call a Brahman priest to marry them in front of a holy fire.

Adultery was a popular pastime in ancient India and daily life offered plenty of opportunities for adventure. The man who delivered corn and filled the householder's granary was invited indoors by his wife, as were the handyman, the cleaner, the labourer in the fields and the door-to-door salesmen of cotton, wool, flax, hemp and thread. While the cowherds enjoyed the cow girls, the superintendents of widows enjoyed the widows in their charge. On warm evenings villagers roamed the streets looking for excitement, while those left at home bedded the wives of their sons.

If a woman visiting the harem pleased the king, one of his wives would tell the woman of the king's love for her and promise her good fortune if she agreed to a secret rendezvous. If she declined to lie with the king, she would be sent away with friendly wishes and gifts.

103

ETERNITY

This position is so-called because of its spiral shape.
Renewing his pledge of love after an absence from home
the man curls his body protectively over the woman's.
This is an intimate, deeply penetrating pose that can be
achieved quite simply. The lovers gaze forwards into the
unknown, shielded from its terrors by their engagement
with one another. She pushes against him with her feet,
indicating separation; he lovingly hugs her to him with
his arms in response.

1 The woman sits on the
floor clasping her knees,
thinking of her lover. In
sadness at his absence she
turns her body away from the
door, bringing her knees
down to her left side and
supporting herself on the
palms of her hands.

2 Her lover returns
  unexpectedly, kneels at
her feet and begins to caress
them. The woman, who has
been weeping, fearing him
dead, half-turns towards him.

3 He moves slowly up her body, caressing her back to life, then embraces her left shoulder and kisses her mouth. She rolls over into the pillows and he enters her from behind, curling his body protectively over hers.

Below: The citizen reassures his wife of his continued ardour after a long absence. She gazes sadly into her loneliness, but in a sign of forgiveness and acceptance, lays her hand on his. Meanwhile, their bodies rejoice in togetherness.

KISSING

The *Kama Sutra* recommends kissing the forehead, eyes, cheeks, throat, breasts, lips and the inside of the mouth. Intense passion may inflame the lover to move on to the joints of the thighs, the arms and the navel. At first, kissing involves the girl just brushing her lover's mouth with her lips. When she becomes less bashful, she may move her lower lip against the lip her lover presses in between hers. When she is aroused, she will shut her eyes and touch his lips with her tongue.

Flirtatious lovers play a kissing game to see which of them can get hold of the other's lips first. If the woman loses, she pretends to cry and protests that they must try again. If she loses a second time, she must take her revenge by getting hold of her lover's lower lip in her teeth and nipping it hard.

Cocoon

Cocoon is a gentle, comforting position that is not too demanding on either partner. This close embrace can lead quite naturally into Butterfly (see page 66).

1 The man kneels on the bed on both knees, squatting comfortably on his heels. The woman sits astride his lap with her feet on the bed behind him and they kiss and caress each other.

2 The man embraces his partner closely, wrapping his arms lovingly round her back. She lifts her feet off the ground and leans back into his embrace, raising her legs as high as she can for the deepest possible angle of penetration. The man rocks her gently back and forth.

GANGES

A difficult pose to achieve, Ganges benefits from yoga practice to give the woman strong arms and a flexible back. The man is in control, but the unusually shallow angle of penetration in the final step means that movement is restricted. Balance and grace are the key here. If the woman tires, move back into Step 3, where the man can support her weight more easily for a return to more vigorous lovemaking.

1 The woman stands erect, feet comfortably apart, arms by her sides. She raises her arms in salutation to the sun, moving them in a wide arc to meet over her head. Then, keeping her torso and arms in line, she bends at the waist and drops her palms to land flat on the ground between her feet. The man moves to stand behind her.

2 The man braces himself with his right leg slightly bent and his right foot forward just inside her right foot. Supporting her weight on her hands, the woman lifts her right foot off the ground and swings her leg up behind her. Her partner rests his right hand under her thigh and helps her lift her leg high until she can lean her shin against his chest, with her foot pointing upwards over his right shoulder.

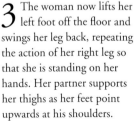

Above: The prince proves his strength, and his lover shows absolute faith that he can hold her. Beware of tiring in this position – the woman's neck is vulnerable to injury.

3 The woman now lifts her left foot off the floor and swings her leg back, repeating the action of her right leg so that she is standing on her hands. Her partner supports her thighs as her feet point upwards at his shoulders.

4 The woman arches her back, pressing her yoni against him and resting her shoulder and cheek against a large cushion. As he supports her thighs and buttocks in his arms, she bends her knees, dropping her feet back towards her head. Leaning her torso against his right leg, she grasps his ankle with her left hand.

RIDING THE ELEPHANT

Indian lovers were nothing if not inventive. This
position is ideal for an intimate session in a howdah, the
ornate canopy that keeps the sun off the elephant rider.
The rolling movement of the beast as it walks along
transmits itself to the lovers, who make no voluntary
movements themselves. The pose can be practised in
the bedroom if no elephant is available.

1 The man kneels with
knees apart and legs flat
to the floor, his toes pointing
straight out behind him. His
back is erect. The woman sits
facing him, astride his lap,
with her knees in the air and
her feet flat on the ground.
The couple embrace. In this
position they can kiss and
arouse each other.

114

2 The man supports the woman's waist in both hands as she guides his lingam inside her. They rest for a moment in this position, while they feel the waves of energy flow between their bodies.

115

3 Now the woman gets into position for 'riding the elephant'. Her right arm circles her partner's left shoulder as she twists her body slightly to the right, his hands still supporting her waist. She curls her right leg behind the man's back and holds it tight against him. His right hand slides down her left leg to clasp her ankle. She supports herself with her left hand on his side. In this position her yoni is tight around his lingam. Small rocking movements prove very exciting, and the man exercises some control by moving his partner's right leg. For more control, he can move his left hand up under her right buttock.

BITING

Not just nibbling but passionate devouring with lips, teeth and tongue and even angry vicious biting were apparently commonplace in the lovers' repertoire of ancient India. Vatsyayana favoured bright strong teeth that would take well to dyeing red or black. He liked to see them even, unbroken and above all sharp. Good teeth could be used to inflict various bites on the lover's skin, such as the hidden bite, the swollen bite, the line of jewels, the broken cloud and the bite of the boar. The left cheek was considered a prime site for biting, as well as the throat, the armpit and the joints of the thighs.

Vatsyayana had a curious idea that if men and women enjoyed biting each other, even the passing of a hundred years would not dim the fire of love.

Below: This love pose is a Tantric classic. Its key features are minimal movement and sustained eye contact. The lovers float into a realm of erotic transcendence where sensation merges with eternity.

117

THE PATH OF LIFE

For this pose, the woman needs a strong, flexible back, and yoga practice will help her achieve it. Once they are engaged, she twists her torso back round towards her lover, who lies behind her. Her hips remain pointing forwards, away from him. With their legs entwined, the lovers look as though they are running together along the path of life. It is unclear from the miniature on page 121 whether they are standing or sitting, but put this down to the artist's fevered imagination. The pose should not be attempted except when lying down.

1 The man lies on his right side on the bed with his right leg bent forwards in front of him and his left leg bent behind him, as if running. The woman lies on her back on top of his right leg. He has his right arm round her back. In this position he can caress her breasts and her yoni with his left hand. Then he clasps her right hand in his left hand and she turns her face to kiss him, cupping his face lovingly in her left hand as she does so.

2 When the time is right, she turns to her right so her back is towards him. She stretches her right leg back between his legs and tilts her torso forwards, bowing her head to his right knee. In this position he can enter her.

3 He draws her torso back up towards him with his right arm, and curls his right ankle under her left knee to anchor her leg to the bed. She brings her left arm up to caress his neck and turns her face towards his. He catches her right knee in his left hand and draws it backwards.

Below: In another pose that would be impossible to achieve without breaking a leg, the artist depicts the lovers entwined on the path of life. Try your own variation lying down.

ORAL SEX

Eunuchs disguised as women specialized in performing oral sex – 'congress with the mouth'. Many were employed in massage parlours. A eunuch giving a man a massage would pay particular attention to his client's upper thighs and abdomen. If the man's lingam became erect, the eunuch chided his client for getting into such a state before proceeding congress of the mouth.

In many parts of India, oral sex was practised exclusively by men on men, but Vatsyayana believed that everyone should act according to their own inclinations. He describes how some men have servants employed to 'suck the mango', while friends do it among themselves. The women of the harem perform the acts of the mouth on one another's yonis, while for many heterosexual couples it provides the ultimate experience of bliss.

121

JACARANDA

This pose begins with close skin-to-skin contact as the
lovers embrace. As the man lies back among the
pillows, their arms and legs entwine spontaneously and
the woman hovers tantalizingly above her lover's erect
lingam. He waits for her to take him before she finally
swoops over her lover's body in a passionate embrace,
her hair flying loose.

1 The woman sits on the
floor with her back
straight and her legs open.
The man sits inside her legs
with his legs over hers and his
feet touching behind her.
They embrace and kiss, and
she closes her feet behind
him. They can stay like this
for a long while, fully aroused.

2 The woman slips her arms down to the small of the man's back, supporting his back as he lowers his torso gently downwards to lie on a pile of pillows behind him.

123

3 He raises his legs, clasping his thighs and holding them open with his hands, and she leans forwards over him, sliding her hands down and helping him support his thighs by holding his knees.

4 Still leaning forwards, the woman brings first one leg back, then the other, so she can kneel with her legs apart and her feet resting on her toes behind her. Then swooping forwards over her lover and pressing his thighs against his torso, she guides his lingam into her yoni. This is a passionate and precarious position, and the woman must take care not to bounce too vigorously, or she will lose her partner.

INDEX

ACKNOWLEDGMENTS

Executive Editor **Jane McIntosh**
Editor **Sharon Ashman**
Executive Art Editor **Leigh Jones**
Production Manager **Louise Hall**
Senior Picture Researcher **Zoë Holtermann**

All photography © **Octopus Publishing Group Ltd/ Mark Winwood**
except for the following:

AKG, London/ Jean-Louis Nou 13 left, 45, 73, 103, 107, 117
Bridgeman Art Library, London/ New York/ Fitzwilliam Museum,
University of Cambridge, UK 7 left, 39, 69, 83, 86 right, 121
/ Private Collection 18, 25, 49, 57, 61, 112 right
The Art Archive/ JFB 93
Thames and Hudson/ Ajit Mookerjee Collection. From 'Sacred Sex'
published by Thames & Hudson Ltd, London, 1997 29 bottom